Playtime

Rockpool Children's Books
15 North Street
Marton
Warwickshire
CV23 9RJ

First published in Great Britain by Rockpool Children's Books Ltd. 2008
Text and Illustrations copyright © Stuart Trotter / Design Concept Elaine Lonergan 2007
Stuart Trotter has asserted the moral rights
to be identified as the author and illustrator of this book.

Printed in China

rockpool
children's books

A Toddlersaurus Book

Stuart Trotter & Elaine Lonergan

Playtime

'Hello.
My name
is Trixy...'

'and it's time to play!'

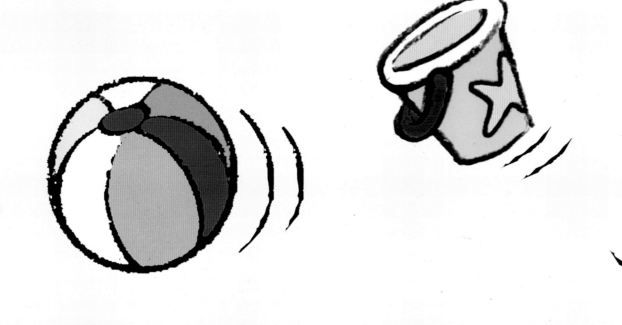

'Watch out, everyone!'
comes the call...

How exciting, what
a sight...

Beach and sunshine, starfish and...

Lots of fun in the sea,

Trixy playing in the sand!

Lift
the
Flap

throw the ball...

One big push,

Lift
the
Flap

see her go...

After a fun

day playing.

it's time to eat

in Toddlersaurus land.....

but that's

another story!